Cat a Plan

written by **LAURA GEHL**
illustrated by **FRED BLUNT**

Ready-to-Read

Simon Spotlight
New York   London   Toronto   Sydney   New Delhi

Here is a list of all the words you will find in this book. Sound them out before you begin reading the story.

Names:

Cat   Dog   Mouse

SIMON SPOTLIGHT

An imprint of Simon & Schuster Children's Publishing Division · New York London Toronto Sydney New Delhi · 1230 Avenue of the Americas, New York, New York 10020. This Simon Spotlight edition June 2020. Text copyright © 2020 Laura Gehl. Illustrations copyright © 2020 Fred Blunt. All rights reserved, including the right of reproduction in whole or in part in any form. SIMON SPOTLIGHT, READY-TO-READ, and colophon are registered trademarks of Simon & Schuster, Inc. For information about special discounts for bulk purchases, please contact Simon & Schuster Special Sales at 1-866-506-1949 or business@simonandschuster.com. Manufactured in the United States of America 0221 LAK

2 4 6 8 10 9 7 5 3

Library of Congress Cataloging-in-Publication Data

Names: Gehl, Laura, author. | Blunt, Fred, illustrator. Title: Cat has a plan / by Laura Gehl; illustrated by Fred Blunt. Description: New York : Simon Spotlight, 2020.
Series: Ready-to-read. Ready-to-go! | Audience: Grades K-1. | Summary: Cat and Dog devise plans to steal a toy from one another, but Mouse comes up with a better plan.
Identifiers: LCCN 2019035959 | ISBN 9781534454101 (paperback)
ISBN 9781534454118 (hardcover) | ISBN 9781534454125 (eBook) | Subjects: CYAC: Cats—Fiction. Dogs—Fiction. | Toys—Fiction Classification: LCC PZ7.G2588 Cat 2020 | DDC [E]—dc23
LC record available at https://lccn.loc.gov/2019035959

Word families:

| "-ad" | → | glad | mad | sad |
| "-ap" | → | clap | map | trap |

Sight words:

| a | and | can | has |
| have | is | | |

Bonus words:

| act | mask | plan | sack |

Ready to go? Happy reading!

Don't miss the questions about the story
on the last page of this book.

Cat is sad.

Cat has a plan.

Cat has a mask.

Dog is sad.

Dog has a plan.

Dog has a mask
and a sack.

Cat is mad.

Cat has a plan.

Cat has a trap.

Dog is mad.

Dog has a plan.

Dog has a map
and a trap.

Cat is sad.
Dog is sad.

Mouse is glad.

Cat and Dog have a plan!

Cat has a mask.
Cat can act!

Dog has a mask!
Dog can act!

Dog has a sack.

Cat and Dog act.

Cat is glad!
Dog is glad!

Mouse is glad!

Now that you have read the story, can you answer these questions?

1. Which characters feel sad in this story? Which characters feel mad? And which characters feel glad?

2. Who do you think had the best plan? Why?

3. In this story you read the rhyming words "clap," "map," and "trap." Those words rhyme. Can you think of other words that rhyme with "clap," "map," and "trap"?

Great job!
You are a reading star!